Katerina
the Cat
and other tales from the farm

Sir Michael Morpurgo is one of Britain's best-loved writers for children. He has written well over 130 books, many of which have been adapted for film, theatre and TV, and won many prizes, including the Smarties Prize, the Blue Peter Book Award and the Whitbread Award. Michael is also the co-founder, with his wife Clare, of the charity Farms for City Children. In 2018, he was knighted for services to literature and charity.

Books by Michael Morpurgo

Farm Tales

BARNEY THE HORSE

KATERINA THE CAT

ALONE ON A WIDE WIDE SEA

THE AMAZING STORY OF ADOLPHUS TIPS

BILLY THE KID

BORN TO RUN

BOY GIANT

THE BUTTERFLY LION

COOL!

THE DANCING BEAR

DEAR OLLY

AN EAGLE IN THE SNOW

AN ELEPHANT IN THE GARDEN

FARM BOY

FLAMINGO BOY

THE FOX AND THE GHOST KING

KASPAR – PRINCE OF CATS

LISTEN TO THE MOON

LITTLE MANFRED

A MEDAL FOR LEROY

MR SKIP

OUTLAW

PINOCCHIO

PRIVATE PEACEFUL

RUNNING WILD

SHADOW

SPARROW

TORO! TORO!

TOTO

WHEN FISHES FLEW

MICHAEL MORPURGO

Katerina the Cat

and other tales from the farm

Illustrated by Guy Parker-Rees

HarperCollins *Children's Books*

First published in the United Kingdom by
HarperCollins *Children's Books* in 2024
HarperCollins *Children's Books* is a division of HarperCollins*Publishers* Ltd
1 London Bridge Street
London SE1 9GF

www.harpercollins.co.uk

HarperCollins*Publishers*
Macken House, 39/40 Mayor Street Upper,
Dublin 1, D01 C9W8, Ireland

1

ISBN 978–0–00–845152–3

A CIP catalogue record for this title is available from the British Library.

Typeset in Times New Roman 13pt/30pt
Printed and bound in the UK using 100% renewable electricity at CPI Group (UK) Ltd

For Freyja and Stanley, your book, your stories.
Happy reading!

Love from Michael and Clare

Contents

I SPY WITH
MY LITTLE EYE

This is how it started, the whole of the rest of

my life.

Our head teacher, Mrs Merton, was

standing on top of the great rock in the middle

of the farm. The wind was nearly blowing her

hat off, and my class were all standing there

looking up at her. And trying to hear what she

was saying.

She was shouting into the wind. 'We're

going for a walk on the wild side. I want you

to look up at the sky, and down at the ground

around your wellies. I want you to look all about

you, and out to sea too. See if you can spot

America. It's out there, two thousand miles

away! Then in half an hour I want us to sit down

behind this rock out of the wind and note down

the five most interesting and unusual things

from nature that you have seen. Not just a list.

I want you to describe each one, each creature,

each bird, each plant, in just a few words. And

try to find something unusual. It's a sort of "I

Spy with My Little Eye". And don't wander off.

There's cliffs all around, and they're very high,

and very dangerous. So

stay close; don't go out of

sight. The teachers have

got whistles. If you

hear a whistle, come

running. Got it?'

My name is Stanley. My nickname was 'Flat' at school, because of a book we all had to read called *Flat Stanley*. I'm twenty-four now, but I was nine years old when all this happened, when we went off from our school on our estate in Birmingham to stay for a week on a farm by the sea in Wales. It was a farm called Treginnis.

I'd never been to the sea before, never been to the countryside or a farm before, never been away from home before. I remember so much of that week. Wind, wind and more wind, racing clouds, driving rain. One moment we'd be

17

herding the sheep, the next clearing up the plastic

from the beach, or milking the goats, or leading

the horses and donkeys out into their field.

Always busy we were, always happy, whatever

the weather.

I didn't know it then, but that walk on the

wild side, as Mrs Merton called it, that next

half-hour changed my life. I've still got the

notebook. Here's what I wrote in it. 'Buzzard

up in the sky high above us. He is mewing like

a cat. Large black beetle crawling through the

grass near my wellie. Spider in a web on a farm

gate wobbling in the wind. Small bird with gold

feathers singing on the yellow bush. And that

was all I could find. Four – I needed five.

I climbed the high rock where Mrs Merton

had just been standing to see if I could spot

something else from up there. And I did. Gulls,

dozens of them, wings outspread, feathering the

wind. They weren't unusual, not at Treginnis –

there were gulls everywhere. But they would

do, I thought. I was fed up. My hands were

cold. Gulls would be my fifth.

That was when I saw it, far out to sea. And

that was when I changed my mind. No one else

was up there with me. Maybe no one else would

have seen it, which would make it very unusual.

I clambered down, found a place out of the

wind, sat down and wrote it down, my number

five. And that's where Mrs Merton found me.

She was looking over my

shoulder as I was

writing. She

asked if she

could see my

notebook.

'Good, Stanley,' she said. 'But your number five – fishing boat bobbing up and down in the waves – it's not really something from nature, is it?'

I said, 'No, miss, but it's unusual, because it looks as if it's leaning over a lot.'

'What do you mean?'

'The boat, miss. It's sort of leaning, like it might topple over any moment.'

'Show me,' she said.

Moments later, I was up on the top of the rock again, pointing out to sea. There it was, the

fishing boat I had seen out near Ramsey

Island, struggling through huge waves

whipped up by wild winds and racing

currents. I knew nothing about

currents then, or how dangerous

those waters could be. All of that

came later. All I knew then was

that the boat was being tossed

about, and couldn't seem to stay

upright.

Mrs Merton stood there staring

at the sea.

'You said it had to be unusual, miss,' I said.

But she wasn't listening to me. She was

already dialling on her phone. 'Police!' she was

shouting over the wind. 'Coastguard! Lifeboats!

. . . I am being calm! . . . Out near the island,

Ramsey Island . . . I am being calm . . . A

fishing boat and it's sinking . . . Mrs Merton, I'm

a head teacher . . . I am being calm! . . .

Treginnis Farm . . . Hurry, please!'

She hung up and turned to me. 'Stanley, you

were very clever to spot that boat. Let's hope

we're not too late.'

26

I could not take it in at first. I knew the

sea was rough, of course, and I could see

the boat was rocking from side to side and

leaning over, but I think I thought that boats

just did that in rough seas. I was bewildered

at her instant reaction – the shouting phone

call, the fear and panic in her voice. I'd

never seen her like this.

She was blowing

her whistle now,

waving her arms,

calling the whole

class over to her and the other teachers too.

Very soon, everyone was up there with us on the

rock, and she was explaining to the whole group

what had happened, how observant Stanley had

been, how she'd rung the Emergency Services,

and how they'd be sending a lifeboat soon. She

told us to keep our eye on the lifeboat station

that we could see on the far side of the bay. And

sure enough, within ten minutes, maybe less, we

saw the lifeboat come sliding down the slipway

and crashing into the sea.

It was so windy up on that rock that some

of us were hanging on to one another in case

we got blown off. We really needed to. None of

us spoke. We just watched as the tiny lifeboat

ploughed its way bravely through huge waves

out towards the fishing boat that was being

driven closer and closer all the time to the rocks

on Ramsey Island.

We saw one of the lifeboat crew throwing

out a line to the fishing boat, but time and again

it fell short, and the crew had to haul it back in,

and throw it out again. It looked impossible and

it looked dangerous. The rocks were so close

by now. The lifeboat was being tossed up and

down on the waves all the time. I never thought

they'd do it, but they kept trying, and finally,

finally they caught the rope and tied it up. And

we all cheered and clapped on our rock as the

lifeboat took the fishing boat in tow and pulled

34

it away. It was slow, but bit by bit they hauled it

away from the rocks, and out to openwater, riding

the waves back towards the lifeboat station.

I was a bit of a hero at supper time, and I liked

that. Mrs Merton said that without Flat – and

she'd never called me by my nickname before!

– no one would have seen the fishing boat, and

the rescue might never have happened. And she

had great news, she said. 'If Flat hadn't spotted

the boat, there would have been no rescue. So

it's all because of Flat that we have been invited

tomorrow afternoon to go down to the lifeboat

station and meet the crew.'

None of us were talking about anything else

that night in our bunks. None of us had seen

anything so exciting. Lives had been saved out

there in front of our eyes. It wasn't on TV. This

was live, and we'd seen it. The lifeboat crew

had risked their lives to save that boat, and we

were going to meet them the next day. I think I

lay awake most of that night.

So there we were the next day, walking

along the coast towards the lifeboat station.

And when we arrived the crew were all

waiting for us. We asked them loads of

questions.

I never heard the answers. I was just

looking at them in their yellow waterproofs

and helmets. I was thinking. I was making up

my mind. They showed us the boat, which

was huge now we were up close to it, and

they gave us cupcakes and juice cartons. And

then the fishermen they had rescued turned

up too, because they wanted to meet us. One

of them hugged Mrs Merton and she looked

quite surprised.

Then a lifeboatman in a peaked cap

was pointing at me and calling me over. He

told me to shut my eyes. I felt him putting a

jacket on me, and a helmet. I heard everyone

clapping and laughing. I opened my eyes. I

was swathed in yellow. I was a lifeboatman.

And I knew from that moment what it was

that I wanted to grow up to be.

Fifteen years on and I'm a fully trained

lifeboatman. I live near the sea and work

nearby, on a farm. If the pager alarm goes off

on my phone, which I always keep with me, I

know it's a 'shout', which means that someone's

in trouble out at sea and there's been a call for

help. I'm in the car at once, and at the lifeboat

station within minutes. I'm climbing into my

yellow waterproofs and wellies and helmet and

I'm ready to go. Then I'm on the lifeboat, and

we're sliding down the ramp into the sea. And

I'm where I want to be, where I belong.

Strange the way things turn out, isn't it?

And everyone in the lifeboat crew calls me Flat.

I like that. I like that a lot.

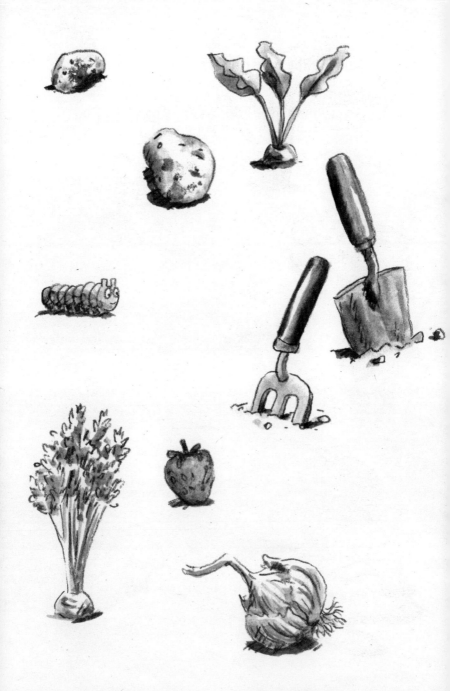

CREEPY-CRAWLIES!

When we got back to school after our trip

away to Treginnis Farm, Miss Humm, our

class teacher, asked all of us to think about the

best thing that had happened during the week,

so that we could either write about it, or paint

it, or both. Over the next few days, many of

us painted or wrote about the same amazing

happening, because it was such a highlight of

the week. For me, especially.

Miss Humm gave us plenty of time for the

project, but told us we should get on with it

whilst everything was fresh in our minds. On

parents' evening, our writings and paintings,

along with the photographs the teachers had

taken, would be put up on display so that the

whole school could share our week down on the

farm at Treginnis. So we had to do our best.

This is what I wrote:

I had a good time at Treginnis Farm, most of the

time. It was a nice place. We had comfy beds,

the ones you climb up on. And I was on the top

bunk, so I could see out of the window. From

my window, I could see the barns on the farm

where all the animals lived: the pigs, the sheep,

the horses, the donkeys, the geese and the hens.

And we could see the house where Dan

lives with his wife and his family. He's very tall

like I am and he's Welsh, so he doesn't speak

like we talk in London. Dan is a sort of farm-

school head teacher, and he looked after us and

we all liked him. I liked the way he spoke too.

I will tell you about our Saturday because

it was the best day I ever had, on the farm or

anywhere. We'd done all our normal work in

the morning, milking the goats, feeding the pigs

and calves. I liked the calves best because they

licked my hand, and they weren't frightened of

me, and I wasn't frightened of them either. They

smelled nice too, milky after we'd fed them.

Not like the pigs, who

smelled like . . .

well, pigs.

Anyway, after lunch we had a job to do in

the vegetable garden. We were supposed to be

digging up potatoes. I never knew

about how you grow potatoes

before I came to Treginnis. I

never even knew they grew in the ground. I

think I thought they just came from Tesco. Or

I hadn't thought about it at all. I'm not sure

which. Dan told us you have to plant a potato

to grow more of them. You have

to put one potato in the ground,

cover it up with lots of earth,

wait a couple of months or something

like that, then you dig

them up. One potato

can make lots. Under just one

plant I dug up twelve potatoes.

But I dug up lots more than just potatoes. I

dug up the biggest worms I have

ever seen. There were all sorts

of creepy-crawlies, like earwigs

and beetles and slugs and bugs. I loved finding

the worms, especially. Every time I stuck my

fork in the ground and lifted some earth, there

were more of them. Wriggly worms and creepy-

crawlies were much more interesting to me

than potatoes. I collected dozens of them in my

bucket.

Dan came to have a look in my bucket and

saw that there were hardly any potatoes, but

lots of creepy-crawlies. He told me they were a

great collection, especially my worms, but that

they would be much happier in the ground and

it would be a good idea to put them back where

they came from, because that was where they

lived, and I wouldn't like to be taken away from

60

my home, would I? He said I should be digging

up potatoes, that we couldn't eat creepy-

crawlies, but we could eat potatoes. We emptied

all my creepy-crawlies back on to the ground,

and we watched them creeping

and crawling and wriggling

away. The worms were

disappearing into the earth

one by one, and it made

me sad to see them go.

But I started to dig up

some more potatoes, like

Dan said.

That was when

it happened. I dug

my fork in quite deep

under a potato plant.

Not a single potato came

up. I got down on my knees, scrabbling about in

the earth to see if I had missed some. Nothing.

Just earth. But then I saw something that wasn't

a potato, and wasn't a stone. It was something

else. Small, round and covered in earth. And it

was yellow. I picked it up and wiped away the

earth. It wasn't yellow. It was gold. It was a

gold ring! Honest. There it was in the palm of

my hand, shining in the sun.

I couldn't help myself – I was shouting my head off. Dan came running, Miss Humm, the teachers, some of the kids. I think they thought I had hurt myself. I held out my hand and showed them. 'It's gold. It's a gold ring,' I told them.

Dan looked at it, and the teachers all had a good look too. The teachers were laughing. 'It's just a curtain ring, Ben,' they said, 'like you hang curtains from. It's brass, not gold.'

Then all the kids were laughing too, and I was feeling really stupid. But Dan wasn't laughing. He was cleaning it with his handkerchief, turning it over in his hand, holding it up to the sunlight.

Then he said, 'I don't believe this. This is amazing!'

And Miss Humm said, 'What? What's amazing?'

And Dan was just laughing and laughing,

but he wasn't laughing at me. Dan was

holding the ring closer to me, trying to show

me something. 'See?' he said. 'Inside the ring

there's writing, engraving. See it? It says:

For my Mary. And there's a date: *28.06.2002.*

You're not going to believe this.'

Then, with all of us standing there in the potato patch, he told us the whole story:

Seven years ago, Mary – her proper name is Mrs Lancaster but we all call her Mary, you know, she does the cooking here at Treginnis – went out one morning to the vegetable garden to pick some broad beans for lunch. There were lots of kids at Treginnis that week, about forty, so she had lots to pick and she was gone a long time. When she came back, she had lots of beans, but she was crying and crying. She had

lost her wedding ring. It had fallen off while she

was picking the beans and she hadn't been able

to find it. She had looked and looked.

Everyone from the kitchen went out to look. Everyone who worked on the farm went out to look. But they couldn't find it. I couldn't find it. The kids looked, all the teachers looked.

A friend of mine who has a metal detector came to look.

Nothing. Day after day, people kept searching.

For years and years, whenever we dug

over the vegetable garden, whenever the

children were planting or harvesting, I looked,

we looked. For all these years we've all been

looking. And now here it is. I can't believe it.

It was all Dan's idea. No one was allowed to

say anything to anyone. We all joined hands

in the vegetable garden and made a promise

together to keep quiet about it. Then we went in

for our supper. Mary and all her helpers gave us

supper in the dining room. We wolfed it down.

We couldn't wait for what Dan said

was going to happen afterwards.

When we'd finished eating, he told us all

to shush, and went to fetch Mary and everyone

from the kitchen and bring them into the dining

room. We were all sitting there in silence,

waiting. Then he called my name. It was all

planned. I knew what was going to happen,

and I was nervous in case I dropped the ring or

forgot what I was supposed to say.

I got up and walked towards Mary, who

was looking a bit puzzled. I could feel the ring

in my hand, deep in my pocket. And then I was

in front of her, looking up at her. All I said was,

'We were digging for potatoes, and we found

this. We think it belongs to you.' I held out my

hand and opened my fingers.

You should have seen her face. It was like

she could not believe what was happening,

what she was seeing. She picked it up out of

my hand. She didn't say a word. She looked

at it, and smiled at me. She was crying with

happiness. Then she put it on her finger and held

up her hand to show us all.

We all clapped and cheered then. The

grown-ups did lots of hugging. And Mary did

a lot of crying. We didn't. We just cheered and

whooped and banged the table and drummed

our feet on the floor.

There was something else Dan told us

that evening after our bedtime story and hot

chocolates – we always had hot chocolate at

Treginnis with our story. 'What you don't know

is that Mary lives on her own now. Her husband

died a few years ago. So the ring that Ben found

in the vegetable garden today means the whole world to her. She told me that this was her best day for a very long time, that we'd all made her very happy.'

Dan looked at me then, sitting there with everyone else in our dressing gowns and slippers. He looked me in the eye, and said, 'You were the worst at digging potatoes, Ben, but the best at digging for gold rings, and for creepy-crawlies.'

KATERINA AND ME, AND KITTY TOO!

My name is Rosa.

I have a tale of two stories to tell you.

First Story

The first thing you need to know is that I am

Ukrainian. I am ten years old, and my home

until recently was in the countryside near Odesa,

not far from the sea in the south of Ukraine. I

lived there on a farm with my mother and father

and grandmother, and Katerina, my cat.

We had cows and pigs on the farm,

and chickens, and mud too, lots

of mud. We grew sunflowers, huge

fields of them. I loved being out with Daddy

feeding the animals, and I loved

going out on the big blue tractor

with him. But best of all I loved

my Katerina.

I must tell you about my cat. Katerina was

quite old for a cat. We don't know how old.

She was originally a stray cat, and she was

black and white and huge. We

did not find her – she found us. She just jumped

in through the open window of our farmhouse

one summer's evening, lay down on Grandma's

chair and slept. She never left. She became

to me the brother and sister

I never had.

My school was just down the road in the

village where most of my friends lived. I didn't

mind school, but I preferred being out on the

farm on the tractor with Daddy, or, even better,

cuddling up with Katerina in my bedroom,

reading a book.

I'd read aloud to her sometimes. I could read

in Ukrainian and in English. Mama was an

English teacher, so she liked me to talk to her in

English, and to read books in English. But when

I read to Katerina, I read in Ukrainian because

she purred louder when I did.

That was my world. Then one day my whole

world changed. The war came suddenly, like a

terrible raging storm. Bombs fell on our barns,

and we ran into the fields. A bomb fell near our

house. One side of it collapsed, just like that.

I wanted to run back to find Katerina, but

Grandma held me tight and would not let me

go. We could see there were lots of houses in

the village on fire, the church too.

Everything happened so quickly. Mama and

Daddy didn't ask me. They

decided between them.

Daddy would stay and

fight, he said. No one

was going to take over

his land, his country,

he said. We would fill

up the car with all we needed, and Mama was

going to drive Grandma and me to the border,

and find somewhere where we would all be

safe.

Everyone was being very calm, except

me. I wasn't calm at all. I couldn't find my

Katerina. I was looking everywhere for her.

Grandma came running after me. She caught

me and held me tight. It was too dangerous,

she said. She wouldn't let me go. I called and

called for Katerina. She never came. I can't

even remember saying goodbye to Daddy. I

remember he said he'd look for my Katerina,

that he'd find her and look after her.

Then we were in the car, Grandma still

holding me tight, me still looking out of the

window for Katerina. The last I saw of home

was the big blue tractor in the yard, Daddy

waving to us, and the flames and smoke rising

above him from the barns.

We were in the car for hours, then queuing

to cross the border into Moldova. Bus, waiting,

train, waiting, bus, waiting, train, waiting.

Sleeping in school halls, in stations, anywhere.

We were cold, so cold I couldn't feel my

hands and feet for days. We were hungry all the

time. But, even then, all I could think of was

Katerina. I kept seeing other people's cats in the cat baskets they were carrying, kept hearing their miaows, and that made it worse.

I was in a daze most of the time. I do

remember the boat across to England, then

arriving and meeting two old friends of Mama's,

from her exchange-student days, she told me.

They were called Molly and Stephen and they would be looking after us. They smiled at me a lot, and they spoke English quite fast, so I couldn't understand that much of what they said. I understood the smiles, though. That was enough.

They lived in a high-up flat in a city called Portsmouth and Mama told me this was to be our home now, for as long as we needed it. We shared one room, Grandma, Mama and me. It was small but we were safe and warm and not hungry any more. That was all that mattered.

From our new bedroom window we could see the sea, but no countryside, just high-rise flats all around and roads and cars.

Within days I was going to an English school where everyone spoke English fast. I had to learn quickly. Everyone was a stranger, and to begin with they would often look at me as if I'd come from outer space. They were all strangers, and I was a stranger too, but not for long. On my birthday – the

101

second of May, and I still don't know who

told them it was my birthday – everyone in the

whole school, teachers too, came in wearing a

yellow and blue ribbon, the Ukrainian colours,

and in assembly they sang 'Happy Birthday'

to me. I felt warm inside all over. I felt I was

amongst friends, that I belonged.

But not a day went by when I didn't think

of home, of the farm, of the big blue tractor, of

my friends. Not an hour went by when I didn't

think of Daddy and Katerina. But here there

were no more bombs, there was no

more war. We spoke to Daddy

on the phone whenever we

could, and he told me he was

still looking for Katerina, that he

was sure she'd turn up sooner or later. He never

talked about the war, and I

never asked. It was less

upsetting that way.

Second Story

Quite soon after I joined my new school in England, my teacher, Mrs Unwin, came into class one morning and told us all that we would be 'going to the farm, to Nethercott'. It turned out that every year my class would all go on a school trip to a farm, for a week or so. It would be springtime, she said. There would be new-born lambs, little calves, bright bluebells in the wood – all very different from city life. The swallows

105

would be back from Africa and we might see fish

jumping in the river. We'd go out working with

real farmers, feed the hens and the pigs, dig in

the vegetable garden, and make ourselves useful

on the farm wherever we could.

'Any questions?' Mrs Unwin asked when

she'd finished.

'Is there a tractor?' I heard myself saying,

daring to speak out in front of my classmates for

the first time. Everyone looked at me.

'You know about farms, Rosa?' Mrs Unwin

asked.

'I lived on one, at home in Ukraine,' I

told her. And then I just found myself telling

everyone about our farm, and about Daddy

being a farmer, and working with him, and also

about the big blue tractor. I said nothing about

the bombing, or the war, and nothing about

Katerina. All of that was private.

Everyone was very quiet as they listened.

When I finished, they were still silent.

Mrs Unwin said, 'Well, Rosa, it will be a big

help to have you with us, won't it? A real farmer.'

A few weeks later, I was saying goodbye to

Mama and Grandma, and Molly and Stephen,

and getting on a coach with Mrs Unwin, the

other teachers and the whole class. They were

all excited, but I think I was more excited than

anyone. I so wanted the farm they were all

talking about to be just

like our farm

at home in

Ukraine. The

tractor had to be

blue and big, and there

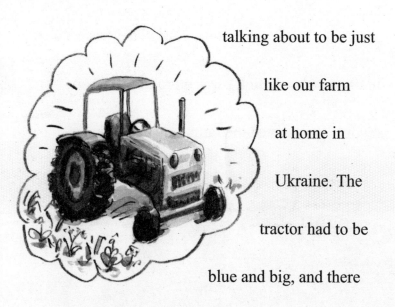

had to be lots of animals,

and sunflowers,

and smells, and

mud. Then I

would be able to

feel at home again,

imagine Daddy was with me, and maybe there'd

even be a farm cat like Katerina. Not that any

other cat could be

like Katerina.

Nethercott turned out to be a huge house,

like Hogwarts from the Harry Potter films.

Only, it was real. Look out of the window of our

dormitory and all you could see were hills and

fields and trees, and cows and sheep grazing.

The fields were smaller than our fields in

115

Ukraine, and there were more hills. But it was a farm, it looked like a farm, and quite soon I discovered that it smelled like a farm too. I felt I was almost home.

And it got even better. When we went out

on a tractor-and-trailer ride the next day with

the farmer to feed the sheep, the tractor was big

and blue! David, the farmer, had rough hands

like Daddy, and he laughed like Daddy laughed.

But I soon discovered there were no

sunflowers. David told me they didn't really have

enough sun to grow sunflowers, and anyway it

wasn't the season. But I didn't mind. Here there

was no war, no bombs. Just peace all around.

I soon discovered something else. Or, rather, something discovered me.

We were grooming horses in the stable yard that first evening when I heard a purring, a purring just like Katerina. It was coming from near my feet. I looked down, and there was a cat, a tortoiseshell cat, but not huge like Katerina. She was called Kitty, they said. And wild, they said, like a wild cat.

She didn't look wild to me. She was winding herself round my boots, all of her purring, tail trembling with pleasure.

People don't purr, I know, but I was as

close to purring then as anyone could ever be. I

reached down to stroke her, and found her tail

stroking me back, stroking my hand.

I was as happy in that moment as I had ever

been at home. Kitty was welcoming me like a

real friend. I found myself speaking to her in

Ukrainian, telling her all about Katerina at home

on the farm, about how much I missed him.

Mrs Unwin must have heard me talking to

her because she was suddenly standing there

beside me, shaking her head. 'I don't believe it,'

she said. 'I've been coming to Nethercott every

year for seven years now. And no one except

you has ever managed to get near that cat, let

alone stroke her. And she loves you to bits. I

think she understands Ukrainian!'

That was the beginning of it. After that,

Kitty followed me around whenever she could.

She wasn't allowed in the house, Mrs Unwin

said. But somehow she got in. At story-time

by the fire that evening, she came and lay

beside me and purred all through the story. Mrs

Unwin made me put her outside. She didn't

dare pick her up herself, and no one else would

either, because she was known for hissing and

scratching you if you tried. She never once

hissed at me, nor scratched me.

Once she even found her way up into

my dormitory and on to my bed. I had one of

those strange dreams that come true as you're

dreaming them. I was dreaming about being

back home on the farm, and Katerina was lying

on my pillow purring. I woke up and there was

Kitty purring like thunder right by my ear!

Whenever we went out to work on the

farm, Kitty would be there. She came with me

into the vegetable garden when we dug over the

potato patch.

She came with me when we went to shut up

the hens in the evening.

130

She came out on our midnight walk when

we went stargazing.

She was there beside me in the field when

we went to check and count the new-born lambs.

It was as if I had a cat-magnet on the heels of

my wellies.

All my friends thought it was very funny,

but I didn't. I just loved it, loved her.

When we were alone, I'd tell her

over and over again in Ukrainian about

my Katerina at home, and Daddy and the

sunflowers. I told her about the bombing

too, and the war and the burning barns and

how much I missed Daddy. It was a great

relief to speak Ukrainian again,

instead of stumbling about in

English with my new friends.

Saying goodbye on the last morning

was always going to be hard. I knew

I'd cry, and I didn't like to cry in

front of the others. As it happens,

I think Kitty must have felt the

same, because I didn't see her

that last morning. She just wasn't

around. I was first on the coach,

138

and deliberately didn't look out of the window

and wave goodbye like everyone else. I stared

straight ahead, holding back my tears, not

talking to anyone in case my voice trembled.

It wasn't until we were almost back at

school, and I saw the parents waiting for us

in the school playground, that I thought at all

about Mama and Grandma, and Molly and

Stephen. They were all there, waiting for me.

We did a lot of hugging as we waited by the

back of the coach to collect my rucksack and case.

Then all of a sudden we heard a scream, a very loud, screechy scream, and a spitting, hissing sound from deep inside the boot of the coach. The scream came from Mrs Unwin, but the spitting, hissing noise sounded like a cat, a very angry cat.

I knew it was Kitty at once. She was crouching in the back, terrified. I was there right away, talking to her in Ukrainian, reaching in and stroking her, the purring echoing in

the big, empty boot. Then I lifted her out, and

introduced her to Mama and Grandma and

Molly and Stephen, and all the time Kitty was

roaring in my ear.

Mrs Unwin rang Nethercott there and then to tell them that Kitty had stowed away in the back of the coach. She walked away and had quite a long conversation on the phone with them. Then she came over and talked to us. 'They say you can keep Kitty, if you like,' she told me. 'They remembered how fond you both are of one another. And she doesn't seem to be fond of anyone else back at Nethercott. What do you think?'

Mama looked at Grandma and at Molly and Stephen, who were all smiling. So was I, and so was Kitty, in her own way.

And that was how a refugee cat met a

refugee me, and lived happily ever after.

Hopefully.

I told Daddy on the phone that same evening

about Kitty, and he roared with happy laughter.

He said how wonderful it will be when Kitty

and Katerina meet, and we're all together back

home on the farm in Ukraine, and we will be,

one day, when there's peace again.

And there will be, he said, there will be.

I hope so. I so hope so.

Farms for City Children

The stories in this book are inspired by school

visits to Farms for City Children.

Farms for City Children was founded in

1976 by Clare and Michael Morpurgo. The

charity offers urban children the opportunity

to live and work on a real farm! Since then

more than one hundred thousand children

have visited one of the farms – Wick Court

in Gloucestershire, Lower Treginnis in

Pembrokeshire or Nethercott House in Devon.

Spending time as farmers brings great joy, new

discoveries and the opportunity to reconnect

with nature, friends and teachers. For many, it is

the most memorable time of their young lives.

You can find out more about coming to stay

on the farms here:

www.farmsforcitychildren.org

LOWER TREGINNIS, PEMBROKESHIRE

Enjoy three more tales from the farm in :

Barney the Horse

Join in the daring rescue of a lost lamb,

meet a boy who saves a family of swallows,

and discover how Barney the horse forever

changes the life of the girl who looks after him.

MICHAEL MORPURGO

Illustrated by Guy Parker-Rees

A FARMS *for* CITY CHILDREN *Book*

Barney
the Horse
and other tales from the farm

ALL SORTS of animals live in the farmyard
behind the tumble-down barn
on **Mudpuddle Farm** ...

Join the fun on the farm, with:

Mossop the old farm cat

Albertine the goose

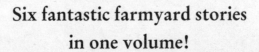

Jigger the sheepdog

Pintsize the piglet

Egbert the goat

and Farmer Rafferty!

**Six fantastic farmyard stories
in one volume!**

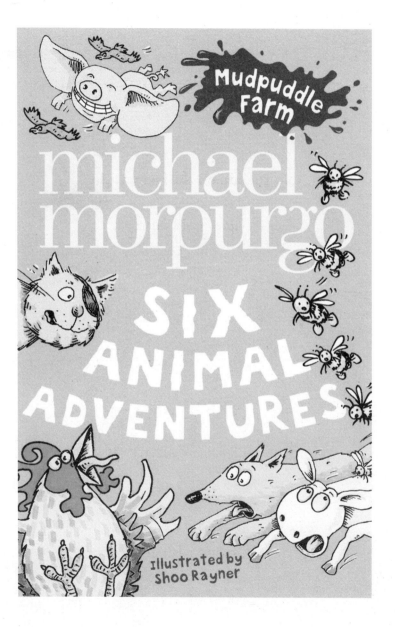

Mudpuddle Farm

michael morpurgo

SIX ANIMAL ADVENTURES

Illustrated by
Shoo Rayner